D1474927

Penny, n.

Penny, n.

Madeline McDonnell

RESCUE +PRESS

Rescue Press, Chicago & Iowa City
Copyright © 2013 by Madeline McDonnell
All rights reserved
Printed in the United States of America

Book design by Sevy Perez
Illustrations by Benjamin Mackey
First Edition
ISBN 978-0-9885873-0-4

Text set in Snell Rounhand LT Std, Adobe Caslon Pro, and
Dawning of a New Day by Kimberly Geswein.

www.rescue-press.org

Thank you DK. Thank you SP and BM. Thank you OED. For longtime support, editorial and otherwise: thank you RX, BL, EL; thank you OFS, JSJ, JP, MB. Thank you KG for reading at a crucial moment. Special thank you to VW. Extra special endless thank you to my rescuer CP. Apologies and thanks(∞) to my superior family. Too much love and never enough thanks to ND, my BP!

Etymology

Penny was pretty.

Or so she'd been told.

As a child, Penny was told of her prettiness often—Sundays, Mondays, holidays. Never mind that the teller was the same. Never mind that the teller was her mother. Penny was only two or three, six or eight. She was not suspicious.

At one year and one month, Penny answered her mother's praise. She responded, finally, to the praise she was fed as regularly, as prosaically, as mashed bananas (Mashed bananas! If only her mother had said, instead, "You are mashed bananas, Penny, mashed bananas." But no—). Her mother floated in the mirror, fumbled a ribbon into Penny's hair. "Pretty," she said, securing it.

Dumbly, Penny replied. She might as well have done so through the bright, unsightly beak of a parrot, or through the lipsticked lips she would maneuver through Latin forms—*pulchra, pulchrae, pulchra, pulchram, pulchra*—years later, the sun slashing the blackboard and burning her arms. But before the mirror, and long before Latin, Penny was young. She had barely made the acquaintance of her mechanic, moronic mouth. In the mirror, it seemed small and sweet.

She looked at it. "Pretty," she said.

She said it again. "Pretty."

It was an act that would have embarrassed a more sentient being. It was an act that possessed an unlucky significance: the first first (along with kiss and love and time) that Penny would later decry. Her first word: *pretty!*

So? It's not as if she knew what she was saying!

Already Penny was a fan of word-music, a little lover of lovely sounds. So she liked her first word's flitty rhythm, that didn't mean she liked its meaning! She might as easily have said *witty* (if only). She might have said *kitty* or *nitty-gritty*. And having so begun, Penny might have become a different woman, a patient fur-petter or a foe of romance, her small sweet mouth set in a flat mean line. She might have become a loose and irreverent cynic (if only!), had she said *shitty*, or *titty*. Or a tar-throated expat with narrowed mascaraed eyes, a Minnesotan-turned-Parisian who wore lingerie that looked like duct tape beneath her soft black clothes. All she would have had to do was wave a wee weary hand, squint a small eye, and croak, *Pas de pitie!* But Penny didn't wave. Penny didn't squint. She looked straight at the mirror and said it. *Pretty.*

So?

It wasn't her idea!

moth·er /ˈmʌð ər/, n.

And it wasn't the only lie her mother would propagate. Throughout Penny's childhood, her mother had imparted several questionable lessons that

9

Penny had nonetheless failed to question. For example: if you keep as still as your Barbie doll your spine will straighten, and your hair will lengthen and lighten, and your waist will shrink, and your legs and breasts will grow. (You'll be 6'3", my pretty Penny! A double-D, a triple-E!) For example: when a woman wants to have a baby all she *really* has to do is keep still. (Well, first she puts on her laciest negligee—yes, yes, just like this one—and then she lies back on her bed like so, with her hair spread over the pillows like this, and her eyelids low and her lashes lush, and then she does it—she keeps perfectly, *perfectly* still—and she waits for the man to come in and climb on her like a kind lion.) And: no, other mothers don't drink Veuve Clicquot with their Golden Grahams, but that's because other mothers aren't as *evolved* as I am. And: yes, other little girls do have to wear girdles just like you, and if Bridey Bridgman says her mother doesn't make her wear one she's lying. And: no you can't play outside, I don't care if Bridey's out there, don't you know she'll like you better if you make her wait? No, I don't care that it's summer—honestly, Penny!—don't you see how sun-kissed your skin already is? Just please, Penny, stay here, keep *still*, look in the mirror. See? One freckle, two freckles, three, seventeen, seventy-three! I named you for all the pretty pennies scattering your pretty little face.

Penny's mother was a widow. Penny's father had "died in childbirth," his heart seizing and clenching, his teeth clenching for good around a lukewarm mouthful of cafeteria brisket. And as his mouth closed around that final, ordinary bite, Penny's mother's legs opened seven floors above. After that, it was just Penny and her mother, for years. Penny and her mother in their penthouse, high in the single skyscraper in St. Paul. Penny's father had made a fortune from a shapewear patent some years before (#4444444, the "cordle," which was neither corset nor girdle but tighter and righter than either, or so the application claimed), and Penny's mother had retired from her job at the public library. Some years later, she had retired to her bed, which was the size of a moderately priced European car. She was tired, she said, so tired. She patted the mattress beside her, tossed a satin sheet in the direction of the far-off floor, so that Penny—who was nearly thirteen, but not yet anywhere near 6'3" or even 5'3"—might climb it like a rope of shiny hair. The nightstand was piled with hairbrushes and hair ribbons, with stubby snuffed candles and tall crystal glasses, with books upon songbooks upon LPs upon songbooks upon books. Once Penny made it into the high bed (this took several minutes at minimum), she would lift *Anna Karenina* from a high stack, and her mother would read the end aloud again (in her mother's version, Anna rips off her dress as she falls to the tracks. Her bare body is a bright light, and the conductor can't help but stop the train).

The bedroom walls were cluttered with mirrors, and, as her mother read, Penny watched her lips move inside the silver. She let the mirrors turn to windows, let her mother's muttering mouth become a fluttering cardinal. Until it was just as her mother had said: they were outside amid soothing birdsong, they were sun-kissed already, and they hadn't even gotten out of bed.

Oh those mirrors were slick and persuasive! They were slippery as the silkiest negligee, they were as dishonest as Penny's mother was deluded. She read Tolstoy and Danielle Steel and Virgil (she liked Book IV of the *Aeneid* best, though in her version Aeneas returns just as Dido lights the pyre, and they make love in the flickering light of its flames) in a voice that was gauzy with falsity, smooth with ludicrous approval. Not surprisingly, all this deceit and delusion—all the lies, all the pretties—led to Penny's infelicitous young womanhood—led—specifically—to her several disastrous affairs.

cord·le /ˈkɔrdl/, n.

Because Penny had assumed romantic luck. No one would abuse her, cheat on her, lie. She was seventeen, twenty-two, twenty-three, twenty-six. She was not suspicious, she was pretty. No one, therefore, would borrow fifty-five dollars and use it to buy fine imported cheeses for a fine imported mistress. No one would call in the middle of the day, requesting pastrami on rye, please, no tomato. No one would ask that she leave said pastrami with a tall, dark administrative assistant—a tall, dark administrative assistant with fashionable eyeglasses, who would later leave several urgent messages on Penny's voicemail. (*Jean-Luc is fucking someone else. Call me back!*) No one would forget her birthday. And no one, oh no one, would, after two months or two years of love, misspell her name. (Peney!?) No one would condemn her misuse of undergarments. Or censure her fondness for the phrase *what have you*. No one would curl his lips at her unwaxed thighs or denounce the precise shade of her pallor. The shade that pervaded each reproachable thigh, each unfreckled cheek, each foot—her back, her hands. Certainly no one would say, after three hard-won years, or even three especially rapturous days, *But I just don't know what love is. I just don't think in those terms.*

Certainly not. Certainly, everyone would look at her as the mirror had, as her mother had. Everyone would cast her silver, flattering gazes. And everyone would say *I love you.*

Years pass. Penny is alone. And Penny is prone to long looks in the penthouse's many mirrors. To befuddled examinations of her mother's blurred compacts. She is prone to scour photos of her early life. Had she even had freckles? But Penny can't ask her mother. Penny's mother is dead. It happened unexpectedly last May, on Penny's twenty-ninth birthday. "Do you know," her mother said that morning, in a dull and unfamiliar voice, "that a woman's fertility begins waning at twenty-seven? Scientifically speaking?" But it was Penny's mother who felt hollow and fallow that day, who heard a cold bell ringing somewhere close, who tasted sterile metal on her tongue. "My throat is so dry," she kept saying, but she refused a single sip of Veuve, no matter how Penny prodded. "My stomach feels scraped," she said. "Will you just leave me alone for a while?" Penny left her alone until the afternoon, and by that time it was too late.

tongue /tʌŋ/, n.

A little over a year later, Penny wakes in her mother's bed with a dry tongue. Has it come? Might this be her own death-day? No such luck. Sun leaks from the edges of the windows like milk from carton creases, and there is a flute of sparkling wine on the book-packed nightstand, one-third full. Penny creaks up, sits for a moment in bed, then lifts the flute and swallows its contents. As a child, she sang songs about champagne. "It's plain as it can be," she sang, staring into her mother's deceived, deceiving eyes, "they thought of you and me, the night they invented champagne." She had assumed romantic luck. And she had assumed champagne to be a necessary component of the life she would lead.

Now, as she ambles to her dressing table—another necessity of romantic young-womanhood—she sees that the essential champagne has left her eyes puffy, and, even worse, has given her left eye a twitch.

She narrows her twitchy, puffy eyes.

At last, she is suspicious.

At last, she looks.

Hair: medium-length, indeterminate in color. Eyes: brownish. She sighs. The champagne flute is empty, the penthouse is empty. The mirror is filled with—what? She looks closer. The problem is: she's spent her whole life this way—humming and glazedly gazing through every unsuspicious morning. She has never questioned the necessity of all these mirrors, of the penthouse's several dressing tables, of the empty bottle, squat in this table's corner. And she has spent every night since she turned sixteen (when her mother told her she'd gotten too big to cuddle and had better get a boyfriend) settling into the crook of some mean man's arm, sighing and crossing her own arms. She has thought, each time, with no variation even in her petulant phrasing: *he doesn't think I'm as pretty as I am.* Until now—the past week, the past month—when there have been, suddenly and without explanation, no crooks, no arms, as few deceitful men as there are deceitful mothers. There is only a mirror, her old reliable, and she looks at it.

The problem is this: she has believed she is pretty, and she is not.

She never has been.

dres·sing ta·ble /ˈdrɛs ɪŋ ˈteɪ bəl/, n.

At first, the mornings are difficult. Penny wakes as before, with her dry mouth, her twitch, but she also wakes with a shock, sitting quickly, snatches of snatched-away dreams (was she still pretty in them?) filming her eyes. "I am plain," she whispers. "Plain Penny." The words stick in her mouth, they are quick but thick. But as she slows her speech and smoothes her voice, as she forces an odd legato—"Plaaaainnnn Pennneeeeeey, Plainnnnnn Pennnneeeeeeeeeeeeey, Plaaaaaaaaaaaaiiiiiiiinnn"—the words begin to make a song. A poem, at very least: Penny composes a heroic line. She repeats it, bleats it, sings it, scans it, takes pride in its lilting but exacting dactylic hexameter.

Hello my name is Plain Penny, I have never been pretty!

Hel-lo-my *name*-is-Plain *Pen*-ny, *I*-have *nev*-er-been *pret*-ty!!

Hēllŏ mў̆ / nāme ĭs plāin / Pēnnў̆ / Ī hāve / nēvĕr bĕen / prēttў̆!!!

With the poem ever in her ears now, Penny wakes to a new sun, and walks past the dressing table without a second glance. She has removed the other mirrors—her mother's mirrors—from the walls, and the room is emptied of its lying silver cast. It is filled with circles, the sunlight printing the carpet with gold polka dots. Penny steps from sun-dot to sun-dot like a child traversing a half-frozen pond. She feels fragile, and yet sturdy, as the floor stays still, as nothing breaks beneath her.

She knows then that she has changed for good, and that—soon, soon—she will find her one true love.

Definition
1) HE IS A LEXICOGRAPHER.

lex·i·cog·ra·pher /ˌlɛk sɪ ˈkɒg rə fər/, n.

But handsome, oh handsome. Penny met him in June. Only sixteen days after her morning before the mirror.

And now they are Penny and Guy. Because seeing in the mirror that she is average has led her to an exceptional thing. To Guy, who is pretty as a girl and handsome as a guy. He is dark-haired. He is exactly six feet tall. His mouth tastes of symmetry—aesthetic, syllabic.

They met at work. Because although Penny had no career, and had, until recently, been fond of saying so ("What do you do?" some mean man would ask; "This," Penny would reply, eyelids low, lashes lush), at the time she met Guy, she went to work each night. She didn't need the money, of course—checks still arrived regularly from the US Patent and Trademark office—but only a pretty woman could justify absolute unemployment. Only a pretty woman could afford to keep so still. So Penny got up, she got out, and she walked six blocks to The Blue Alligator.

She supposes she was hired for her name. Because the bar was run by another Penny, an older Penny known also as Pen. This Penny had inky hair and winky eyes, glittery with anticipatory vindication. She wore shiny blouses that let slip every secret of her décolletage: that it was constrained by bras of surprising color, that it was powdered in metallic shadow, that it was extraordinarily large. Penny felt like a middle-school girl in Pen's presence, reviled for her flat chest. She felt bad. And she was bad—knocking Knock-Out Punches on the silken ties of foreign business men, forgetting to dot their drinks with orchids and paper umbrellas, forgetting their hot salted Brazil nuts, breaking tiki glasses and cutting her fingers on shards. At some point each night, she would lock herself in the one-stalled, electric blue bathroom. She would sit on the cracked toilet seat and reprimand her skirt. You're blue and scaly! You're too short! She'd pull, but the skirt would not stretch.

She stayed because, on Tuesdays, Pen let her sing. She had always wanted to sing, or so she'd claimed when Bridey had proclaimed, through their youth, "*I* want to be a marketing director or maybe a day trader." Anyway, the dream had come true. At least it seemed to have, each Tuesday, as she stooped over the mic, warbling, "Someday he'll come along," just as her mother had taught.

Of course her mother had also maintained that someday the man *would* come along. But there were no men most Tuesdays. No men who spoke English, at least. Pen had finagled The Blue Alligator into several tourist guides, so there were foreign men with large hands and manicured fingernails, white-haired men with gigantic, uncomprehending smiles and beautiful, navy suits. Otherwise, there were just Pen's sisters and Pen's bridge club and Pen's blowsy friends, with their falsified, colored-on hair.

Until one Tuesday.

Penny stood at the microphone. She'd gained weight since she'd looked herself and her mirror straight in the face—switching from champagne to an old woman's sweet sherry—why worry about the puff or the caloric content or the twitch?—but she felt light. She did not worry about the red veining her left iris, or her waterlogged eyelids. She did not worry about her short skirt or pallid thighs. Why worry? She wasn't pretty anyway. So she didn't stare at her shaking, freckleless hands, or at her round knees. She just closed her eyes. And sang with all her heart.

"Maybe I shall meet him Sunday, maybe Monday, maybe not. Still I'm sure to meet him one day. Maybe Tuesday will be my good news day."

She paused and took a breath. She blinked, and there he was.

He was looking from her feet to her knees to her mouth. From her mouth to her eyes to her forehead.

He was looking at her as if following the hopeful motion of her notes, the hopeful meaning of her words, his gaze going up, up, up, to the lights. They made his eyes so blue.

She took him home with her. She was thirty, after all—not young. And it was June, and hot. Her electric blue blouse stuck to her back.

She offered him a drink. A champagne flute filled nearly to the brim with syrupy Harvey's Bristol Cream. Guy choked on the first sip. It didn't matter. She was floating, she was blown about the humid room. And Guy looked at Penny now as if following her breezy progress, eyes darting from cheek to earring, from ceiling to coffee table. His eyes, which were intent, uncluttered, and so blue even still. It hadn't been a trick of the barlight.

Penny had never liked to be looked at, not even in her pretty days, but now—oddly, marvelously—she felt not the accustomed discomfort—but an unfamiliar, delicious relief. She was relieved, she realized, to feel her shoulders slump. She was relieved to feel her colorless hair dampen and curl about her brow, to feel it flatten, unattractively, against her scalp. Guy looked at her like a man in love! And yet she knew what he saw was not pretty. What he saw was not physical, not substantial. It was the light that had rayed from her since her morning before the mirror, beamed from her even in the blue bar, the dark taxi, the dim elevator.

Guy saw it. Her unburdened and unburdening light, her lightness. Her prepossessing disappointment, her intoxicating engagement with reality, her utter lack of expectation.

He inched closer on the couch. Coughed. "What do you do?"

"Um?" She shifted.

"For work, I mean."

"You just saw it."

His uncluttered eyes cluttered. But then, dashingly, they emptied out. "You get paid for that?"

Penny nodded.

"Hunh." Guy sipped his Harvey's, choked quietly.

"I didn't realize that sort of thing was so... remunerative."

"What do you do?" Penny asked.

"Pen didn't tell you?"

"Pen?"

"Oh yeah, I know Pen, she's been nagging me to go to her club for a while—she thinks I don't go out enough." He grinned an incandescent grin, raised his fingers in delicate air-quotes. " 'Social anxiety.'" He laughed, and deftly waved the phrase away. "Yeah. Pen's sweet," —Pen: *sweet?*— "she worries about me, even though we haven't known each other long. We met last year, at a one of those PEN American 'Eat Drink and Be Literary' things."

"Pen is a member of PEN?"

Guy smiled. "Well, not really, as it turns out. But she liked the name."

"So you're a writer?"

Guy flushed. "Oh no. But I love—" he paused (was he choking again?) "—language."

He was a lexicographer. But handsome, oh handsome. Indeed, as Penny would discover, there was no way Guy was a writer. Writers were gnarled and hunched. They had lined faces and whiskeyed voices,

27

eyes cluttered with insight and sadness. Guy watched Penny with mouthwash eyes, Jacuzzi eyes. He watched himself too—intently, piercingly. He was extremely fond of watching himself, as it turned out. He was extremely fond of unwriterly reflective surfaces.

That night, rising to use the bathroom—and to dump his Harvey's in her bathroom sink before popping a passel of Paxils—Guy paused in the living room, for one, two, three, four, five, six seconds before one of Penny's old reliables. One of her *remaining* old reliables. She had taken them all down, but then the walls were so bare... She re-hung three, maybe four, the ones with the prettiest frames. *She* didn't have to look at them.

But Guy did. Guy turned his face to the left. He turned his face to the right. He stroked a sideburn.

Oh no, Penny thought, and just as I've broken free!

But by the time Guy emerged from the bathroom, she'd forgotten his vanity. He was looking at her. She couldn't move.

"You're very hard to talk to," he said. So he looked at her. He looked and looked.

2) IT IS NECESSARY TO DESCRIBE THE RAPTURE THAT FOLLOWED.

rap·ture /ˈræp tʃər/, n.

Because, though they wouldn't stay, those were the happiest days of Penny's life. Days that began in bright mornings and lengthened into blue-white afternoons. Days beginning with Guy, in his boxers, standing over her toaster, spreading honey on the hot slice that curled like a leaf in his hand. "I had the weirdest dream," he would say, as she slipped into the kitchen, as she pulled her robe tight around her waist. "It was awful actually because it was the summer before my parents' divorce again, so I must have been twelve. Which is weird, because my girlfriend from college was there too, and she was *pregnant*, which, obviously, I was upset about..." Guy continued, but Penny couldn't hear. She had pulled her robe tight, but then Guy had pulled at its sash, and now his arms were tight at her waist, his nose in the vicinity of her left temple, his words muffled by her hair.

Afternoons, he paced the penthouse, stomping on the ragged hems of his jeans. Did she mind if he worked here? He worked remotely anyway— the main office was in England and he'd had visa problems, not that he'd fit in very well there anyway ("the *Marmite*!" he explained)—but his place was so lonely, so lowly, so low (it was a basement apartment, for which Guy paid $360 a month), and did she mind? No. Oh no. So Guy set his laptop on her dressing table, and stood over it, tapping out definition text, the white screen spotlighting him, smoothing and silvering his skin, making him a midcentury movie star. Oh! He was lovely as a girl, handsome as a guy—Penny didn't blame him for his fixation on the mirror. Besides, he watched himself intently but innocently, with an air of easy blame-lessness. He smiled at himself in the computer screen, and in the beveled mirror, and spun away.

He took her back to bed. He held her through afternoons that spun in circles, blue and white as china plates.

Looking back, Penny sees that she should have known. That it couldn't last. That it couldn't—that it shouldn't—have been so easy and unspecific. But it's too late. She lies sleepless in autumn light that is pale green—like sea-foam or celery or—ugh—like the freeze-dried marshmallow shamrocks in Guy's morning cereal. (He never rinses out the bowls, just leaves them on the table, filled with piebald milk.) Anyway, Penny thinks, that's what love is, at first. That's what love is, at best. It is wonderful *because* it is unspecific. It is wonderful *only when* it is un-specific. And it is really, absolutely wonderful only when it is really, absolutely unspecific, as it was with Guy in June. Only later did it become as descriptive and definitive as Guy's best dictionary text.

Cruel trick of evolution! Because anyone able

to see through that vague initial haze would not fall in love in the first place. Anyone and everyone endowed with such x-ray vision had to have died out. Like brontasauri. Like thicktail chubs or stumptooth minnows, their fishy skeletons stuck at the bottom of the sea. Like woolly mammoths or long-tusked, woolly rhinos. Like Shakers. As a child, Penny had gone to a summer arts camp in New Hampshire. She fingerpainted self-portraits, and tried her hand at the lute, and, at night, she was herded, along with the others, into the Shaker village where they were expected to sleep. She remembers the wooden bed, the fallen ladder of the headboard. It was unpainted, bare and barren as its makers. It was all right angles, and she couldn't sleep. She just stared at the bare wood, riddled with scratches, as if someone long ago had grasped and clawed at it, begging for clemency.

Next to Guy now, she tosses, then moves close. She touches her lips to his slick trick of a neck.

3) BUT AT FIRST IT SEEMED A LUCKY SHIFT.

shift /ʃɪft/, n.

August came, and then September, and Penny was happy. In fact—at first, at foolish first—Penny was happy to have inveigled her way out of their initial vagueness, happy to know that this was not just infatuation, this thing with Guy. He looked at her, still, with light in his eyes, but now there were other things there too: detection, recognition. Identification, affinity, knowledge.

But what did Guy identify? What did Penny know? What did Guy and Penny have in common?

Well...

A history with mirrors, at very least.

And...

And?

A love of language! Yes! Because, though she'd neglected Virgil and Tolstoy and Steel since her mother's death, Penny still attended tenderly to the words in the songs she sang (*we'll build a little home, just meant for two*)—their touching fidelity to formal usage (*from which we'll never roam*)—their chiasmi (*who would, would you?*). She loved their simple, tongue-twisting rhymes (*either, aye-ther, neither, naye-ther*), their similes (*naïve as a babe, normal as pie, bromidic and bright as a moon-happy night*). And Penny loved these words more now than ever. Because it was September, but she *was* corny as Kansas in August and she *was* high as a kite on the fourth of July. Though August had come and gone, and July before it. On the fourth, Penny and Guy had lain together on the blanketed bed, all the windows open. The bed sloped like a lawn, and outdoor air filled the room, and it didn't matter that they couldn't see the firecrackers.

Guy didn't love Penny's songs—those over-familiar lyrics that she nonetheless felt she'd invented (*I expect every one of my crowd to make fun of my proud protes-*

tations of faith in romance)—but he did love words like *bubble tea* and *Klonopin, chupacabra* and *triple-double.* He was a lexicographer. He loved lemmae.

She liked it when he talked about his work. At the end of August, he'd sat at her kitchen table, the laptop screen soaking his face in an approximation of moonlight. "It can be frustrating," he said, "because I get attached to my lemmae. They're like friends, kind of." He looked at her, despondent. "And what's to separate a word like *chowhound,* or—" spitting, "—*bouncebackability,* for God's sake, which, believe it or not, old editor Nigel claims 'has attained a level of currency that merits inclusion' from *amigurumi* or *carbon-neutral* or *insourcing*?" He threw up his hands, half-stood, then collapsed in his chair. "We've got *outsourcing.* I mean, come on! We've had *outsourcing* for ages." He stood, knocked the chair back. Walked to where Penny stood at the stove, stirring pappa al pomodoro with a wooden spoon. Pressed a desperate, clammy hand to her cheek.

"I love *insourcing,*" he said—and her heart fluttered—her heart became a bromidic, beating bird because, dear God, he'd just made a declaration. He *loved* insourcing. ("It's so efficient!") *Loved* it. She dropped her eyes, gazed bashfully at the floor.

"Of course," she said.

They'd both been susceptible. Because if a word as antiseptic as *insourcing* could induce true love in him, could set even her own unexpectant heart aflutter, who knew what warmer words might do? Who knew what destruction words like *dear* or *lover* or *kitten* or *darling* might wreak?

4) BUT IT IS DIFFICULT, NOW, TO REMEMBER HOW THE NAMES BEGAN.

names /neɪmz/, pl. n.

After all, their relationship was once so unspecific as to defy memory. It was once ill-suited to specific monikers, if ideally suited to lust, that most intrinsically vague state. They lay together in the dark bedroom, and Penny gazed at Guy, as through an appropriately amorphous fog. She reached through the haze, seeking something solid, and, invariably, he pulled her close. It would have been strange then, caught in his arms, to have called him "My Little Papa Smurf" or "Gleegle T. Beagle" or any of the other tragically specific inanities that have since invaded their discourse. It would have been strange to have called him by any name at all. Even Guy.

Guy. If only she could say the word now. That simple, single syllable. When did she say it last? This morning she has called him "Guy Foxy" and "My Old Faithful Geezer-Geyser," but when was he last—when was he just—ah yes—

They were sitting in bed. It was early September, early morning. Indian summer, the outside sky cloudy, the bedroom dark. "Guy?" she said. But what was it she'd wanted to ask? She doesn't know, just sees herself, supine then as now, her eyes dim but wide, blankly inquiring. "Guy?"

As if to ask: who are you? Who are you, really?

(But had she really wanted to know?

Had she wanted to know, for example, that Guy lost his virginity at only fourteen, to Yuki Swenson, who was seventeen, who was half-Swedish-half-Japanese, who lived in a columned house with a finished basement, who led Guy by the hand down its soft, carpeted stairs that fateful Friday, who turned the volume on the Nintendoed TV all the way up, all the while smiling slyly? Did Penny want to know about the smell of fryer oil that had pervaded the basement because Yuki's little brother Haruki hadn't thrown away that afternoon's McDonald's wrappers? Did she want to know that Guy had timed his thrusts into Yuki's smooth body to the Super Mario music boinging endlessly from the frozen screen, that, at times in college, Guy had put the video game on the tiny TV in his dorm room, hoping to repeat this trick on Katie Mancini or Jessica Gomez or—most often—Mindy-Lou Howe?

Did she want to know, alternately, about the summer Guy's father left, the sweltering Saturday morn-

ing when Guy found his mother crying in the back-
yard garden, the bitter bilious sickness that filled him,
the disgusted lecture he then delivered to her, his be-
reft mother, about "inner resources"? Did Penny want
to know that he'd shared a bed with his mother several times that summer, even though he was thirteen
already and almost six feet tall, even though he had
hair under his arms and boxer shorts, even though he
was fond of lifting the band of those boxers when he
lay awake in his own bed, of inspecting that still-soft
hair, of petting it and ruffling it the way he petted
and ruffled his Great Pyrenees, Søren Kierkegaard?

Did she want to know that the dream Guy had
tried to tell her about, the dream of Mindy-Lou's
pregnancy, wasn't a one-time thing, that he had this
dream once a month at least, that he'd had it at least
seven times while sleeping next to Penny, in the bed
that also was, still and always, her mother's deathbed?
Did Penny want Guy to admit that the first time he'd
entered her penthouse he'd imagined striding past her
to the wall of windows at the far end of the living
room, of lifting, of climbing, of leaping? Did she want

to know about his therapist's favorite theory, the one about how his parents' divorce had come at a problematic time with regards to Guy's "sexual coming-of-age," that the trauma had "stunted" his "relational development," that he might always be too, ahem, immature for the work of real romance? Did she want to hear that Guy was less concerned about his romantic midget-hood than he was about the bleak and seemingly sourceless grief that sometimes filled him, a bleak grief he combated with a silent recitation of morbid puns (he liked the one about the cannibals and the clown best; *does this taste funny to you*, he would repeat, *does this taste funny to you does this taste funny to you does this taste funny*) or Paxil? Did she want to know that the bleak grief had once visited him while he was watching her perform "their song" (*maybe Wednesday, maybe not...*) at The Blue Alligator? That he'd risen from his stool before she'd even reached the bridge, that he'd actually crushed up one of his Paxils and snorted it from the gooey blue top of a toilet tank?

Really?

Did she want to hear every bloody secret, as Guy's

old editor Nigel might say, every *bodily* secret? Did she want to know about the puce mucus Guy had stuck to the bottom of her dressing table as casually as raspberry gum? Did she wish to witness the discus-thrower's pose Guy sometimes adopted when he felt an especially violent emission of gas coming on?

No? *No?* Well then! What on earth was she—almost—asking?)

"Yes, Penny?" Guy rolled on his side, propped his beautiful jaw with one hand. He looked at her, his elbow sunk in the pillow. "You know, you don't really look like a Penny."

Aha! No matter what Penny did or did not know, no matter what Penny did not, could not, ask, Guy knew her—Guy saw what even her mother hadn't. She smiled. "No freckles, right?"

Once again the clear eyes cluttered. Once again, they emptied, debonairly, out. "Freckles? You want me to call you Freckles?"

She shook her head.

"Well, what should I call you?"

A silly question, simple as his one-syllable name.

A moment of inconsequence. She didn't ponder or protest. "What would you like to call me?" she asked, instead.

He enumerated the possibilities. Conventional, at first. Mildly comic, but ultimately unobjectionable. All the while, he stroked her face sweetly.

"Beautiful? Baby-cakes? Babykins?"

"Mm. I don't know." As a child, she had wished her name were Gwendolyn.

"Doodle-bug?"

Gwendolyn, how about Gwendolyn?

"Shabookadook?"

Perhaps now, at last, Gwendolyn, but—

"Duchess?" he said. "Gum-drop? Honey-toast? Lamby-pie?"

"Are you hungry or something?" Gwendolyn had worn gauzy clothes. She had worn her hair always up, even while she slept.

"Snooky? Winky-dink?"

She shook her head.

Later, giving up, she nodded off. Or had she nodded, by mistake? Whatever the case, she's not sure now how he settled on "Yeti," which became "Confetti," which turned, later, to "Coco T." Because at first, he called her Penny, too. There was a balance, after all, between affection and realism, between detection and clarity, between tenderness and the increasing violence of autumn, the quick cold that clamped the windows shut and kept them, more and more, inside.

Besides, she liked the names. Sometimes. Some of them, at least. "Apricot" and "Angel-puss" and "Twinkles." "Squidgy" and "Star-sweeper" and "Cloth-ears" and "Duck." For a week in early October, he was stuck on "Krazy-Little-Kitty-Kat," or "KLiKK," and she found herself mewing in response, curling her painted fingernails into Krazy-Little-Kitty-Kat-Klaws (KLiKKKs), scrabbling at his flannel. But why? She was thirty now—not young. She accepted it—she was a plain-old, plain adult, and yet she could not stop kidding, like a giddy, pretty girl. That word— *kid*—made new sense. She kidded and then *was* a kid, curling and purring against Guy's sweater as she had against her doting mother's chemise, batting at Guy's scratchy, yarny stomach, licking her palms and

43

dabbing at the lipstick she'd left on his cheek.

But kids don't wear lipstick. And Penny—who'd worn it since she was sixteen, who'd stayed faithful to the stuff even upon realizing that the mouth it enhanced was disproportionately puny—barely wider than a nose!—started forgetting to smear it on. What was the point? She wasn't pretty, and Guy was touching her less and less. It was cold, it was autumn, the moon appeared earlier now, a silver curve in the sky. Lust was better suited to summer, to its thick darkness, its simmering hush. Now, the sun rose, and they lay side by side in its broad glare, and Penny opened her eyes not to Guy's touch, but to the bright, cold light, and to the sound of him.

"Good morning Ducky, good morning little Abominable Yeti-liebchen, good morning my friendly Fur-ball, good morning Clam-digger, and Crumpet, and Chickabiddy, and Sheepy-lamb."

"Ba-ah-ah," she responded, "ba-ah-ah-ah!"

"Oh good morning, Munchkin and Muffin and Muppet and Muggles."

"Good morning."

"Give me a huggles, Muggles!"

Because, yes, there were huggles still, huggles in abundance. No matter that it was growing even colder, that it was nearly November, that there were few kissles, fewer caressles, and fewest fuckles.

"Good morning little Cherub, little Yuppy-puppy! Are you a very good puppy? Should I scratch you behind your little cuppy-puppy ears? Should we get uppy, my bestest, nicest puppy?"

Oh, why?

Why?

She was an adult, a woman, and yet she couldn't cease this kidding, this crittering. She was a human, and yet she was mewing and yipping, bubbling her mouth like "Goldy T. Goldfish." She was thirty. And yet, there was something compelling about this search for her proper, crittery name. She clucked like Penny-Henny, she screeched like Delphine Dolphin, and Guy looked at her.

For a moment, his eyes uncluttered. No detection, no knowledge of her Penny-ness, of her shameful fondness for treacly lyrics, for words *as trite and as gay as a daisy in May*. No detection of any of her many imperfections, no knowledge of a single specificity. Yes: for a moment, for just a moment, Guy looked at Penny the way she looked at him.

Anyway, this was probably just a phase.

It wouldn't (it couldn't!) get any worse.

5A) IT GOT WORSE ON NOVEMBER THIRTEENTH.

worse /wɜrs/, adj.

A Friday. Yeah, yeah—most ill-starred of days, she should have known—but he just seemed so—happy. He emerged from the bedroom. Penny stood at the sink.

"You'll never believe it!"

She turned. His hands were in the air, his face was

flooded with—with—

"*Nigger!*" He hopped from one foot to the next. "What!?"

"*Nigger! Nigger!*"

Dear God! Why this? What was wrong with "Apricot," with "Muffin," with "Itty-Bitty-Standy-Sitty—"

But he was talking again. His hands were on her waist, his voice was low. He repeated the horrible word. Then: "They've given it to me."

"What?" Cold air blew against the window. Blue leaves pressed the panes. His breath was hot on her forehead.

"*Nigger.*" He whispered it, his voice caught by a low, sweet fever.

Her own voice came out small. "Why do you keep saying that?"

"Because it's mine now! I'm going to define it, revise it, I mean." He took his hands from her waist, busied them at his sideburns. Blinked. "And, jeez, Penny—"

Penny? Had he actually just called her—

"Penny, jeez. You don't know what an honor this

is. It's such a complex word—the history, the tricky modern usage—and, well, to be the one to revise that—that—woefully inadequate tripe we have now—" He walked backward, fell into a chair.

"That's great, Guy," and—why, that was it, actually—the last time she'd said his name. She smiled. She was suddenly unsuspicious, emboldened. He'd called her Penny!

"Great," she repeated.

How could she know what was coming?

5B) OH GOD, WHAT WAS COMING.

God /gɒd/, n.

He turned the bedroom into a study. His own bedroom-study eight blocks north was "too messy," and well, actually, his therapist thought it was a really good sign that he'd begun "embracing domesticity" this way, and, well, he sort of agreed, maybe? And, well, maybe this "routine they'd established" would help with his anxiety problem, a problem which proved particularly problematic whenever a large assignment loomed? Either way, her bedroom (her mother's bedroom, her mother's deathroom), with its streaked windows and dirty, watery light, its art deco furnishings and dusty, empty champagne bottles, was now his.

The floor was a checkerboard, stacks of paper quadrangling this way and that. He sat on her bed. She made her precarious way toward him, nearly tripping over piles of papers large as sitting babies (maybe soon they would have babies, she and Guy?).

"Guy?"

He didn't look up.

"Sweetums?" she tried. "Very wonderful Itty-Bitty-Kitty-Keeper?"

He raised his head and blinked. His eyes were owly

and strange, his face pale as a vampire's. "Hunh?"

"You want some dinner, my wondrous Muffin Man, my Papa Smurf, my very reliable Lamb Shepherd, my trusty Shepherd's Pie?" She tried this more and more often, employing an increasingly maniacal tone. Thinking that, if she mouthed it to alienating excess, his rhetoric would soon lose its charms.

"You know, KLiKK," he said, "these primary sources are really fascinating. I mean, I know how this sounds, but it's true. At least in some cases."

"What's true?"

"Some slaves really did love their masters."

She had arrived at the bed. She had braved the uneven floor, its trick checkerboard. Still, Guy seemed far away, floating among the pillows. She glanced behind her. The paper-stacks looked like whitecaps. She turned back.

Guy rubbed his eyes. Like a baby. A baby— maybe someday, maybe soon, it had to be soon, she was thirty after all, maybe now, yes now!—but what was it she'd wanted to say? Oh yes, dinner.

But Guy was saying something, not "dinner" but "love." (Love!) "Loved them," he said. "Listen to this: 'I truly loved my master's face. It held a kind white light, which shone always, more even and tender than the sun.'"

Penny hovered. It was her bed, and yet it seemed to float away. The floor lurched. "That's ridiculous."

"Of course it is, but it's still interesting, and this is a fairly reliable source, verbatim accounts, and—"

"But why are you reading them? Why do you want to read that stuff?"

Guy shrugged. "Just looking for early citations."

November air seeped through the closed windows and touched her skin. Dinner. She'd meant to say dinner. She'd meant to climb onto the bed, to crawl to him, to lift his hands from the keys, place them on her neck, her shoulders, her breasts. But she stood unmoving on the frozen, hardwood sea, the white waves of papers suspended behind her in furrowed procession. The cold touched her, but Guy wouldn't. Not that she was in much of a mood to touch Gleegle T. Beagle or Old Faithful Geezer-Guyser (though a quickie with Guy Foxy sounded okay), but did she have a choice? She was going to be thirty-one. Soon! Sooner every day. A woman's fertility began waning at twenty-seven, scientifically speaking...

Anyway, whether or not she wanted him, she wanted him to want her. She knew she was plain, was happy to be plain, but did that mean she had to be happy to be a mangy kitty, a disgusting mutt? *Disgusting.* She tried to slow and smooth the word, to force an odd legato—Disguuuussstinggggg-disguuuuuuuustinggggg—but still she heard no poem, no song. She closed her eyes, still trying. "Disguuuuuuuuuuuuuuusssssssssstttinnnngggggggg."

"What?"

"Um. Disgusting?"

"Oh, come on, Kit Kat, it's just research."

"Still." She paused, caught her breath, her thoughts. "It's, it's disgusting! I wish you'd never been assigned that horrible word. I wish you'd go back to *mack daddy* and *pity party* and *emo* and *con-*

flict diamond and—"

Guy smiled. "Relax, Reeses-Pieces-of-Pudding-Pot-Pie." He put the laptop to his side, knelt on the quilt. "You should read these, actually—they're surprisingly moving. Of course it's totally fucked up, but there's real devotion here and—" He looked at her. "Anyway, don't you identify, just the littlest bit? Don't you think you're sort of like my little bitty kitty slave?" He began toward her, crawling over the quilt. She felt her skin tighten, her waist cinch. "Don't you think you really are such a very good loyal slave to your nice, nice, kind, white master?"

"You *are* looking pale," she rasped. He had barely left the bedroom-study all week.

But he moved now. He was close, and coming closer. Soon he would kneel at the foot of the bed, and press his nose to hers, his mouth.

"Hey there, little Slavey-kins."

She was turned on. "Hey," she said. And she turned on. "Hello, Master."

5C) MASTER.

mas·ter /ˈmæs tər, ˈmɑ stər/, n.

That was Guy. Penny was Slave. Slavey-kins, Slave-ocula, Slave-bear—the stem was always the same.

Slave! Sometimes she was philosophical. Oh well. She'd never much liked her name. (And wasn't this new name better than those others? Didn't it at least allow for the possibility of sex? Even Thomas Jefferson had fucked his slaves!)

But sometimes she couldn't take it.

5D) SO SHE WENT TO WORK.

work /wɜrk/, n.

Maybe that was the solution! She had her own life to live! Her own work to do! She would lose herself in it: in work, and song.

Wasn't that what good little slaves had always done? *Lord, I keep so busy servin' my Master, keep so busy servin' my Master, I ain't got time to die!*

But work was horrible. Penny had missed too many shifts during that early blue-white time, those first days of Guy. So Pen had stopped speaking to Guy, and—worst of all—Pen had put a stop to Penny's singing. Days like today, a Tuesday, were, as often as not, karaoke nights, and Penny had no choice but to stand in the bar's back shadows, an aquamarine dish towel draped over one arm, watching the foreign businessmen.

Who twisted their eyes closed, who leaned back, endlessly screaming, *Bennie, Bennie, Bennie and the Jets, Bennie, Bennie, Bennie, Bennie, Bennie and the Jets. Bennie, Bennie, Bennie, Bennie, Bennie, Bennie and the Jets!*

Except they were foreign men with slender hands and beautiful ties, and their English was inexact. They sang and screamed, and tonight it sounded like: *Penny, Penny, Penny has the shits, Penny, Penny, Penny, Penny, Penny has the shits. Penny, Penny, Penny, Penny, Penny, Penny has the shits!*

And so—what else could she do?—Penny quit.

She handed Pen the blue tray, the blue dish towel. "I—I've got to get out of here. So. I—quit?"

Wait, what? What had she said? She hadn't managed to say as much to Guy, but here it was, that sudden elegant word, slipping from her mouth. *Quit!* Such a quick, lovely sound. And Pen didn't even mind. Pen just grinned victoriously. Pen just nodded—then intensified her nodding, as if listening to a lecture that was veering on brilliance—and asked that Penny return her blue uniform. She actually called it that: "Don't forget to return your blue uniform!"

Ah! *I've been givin' my all, I've been servin', and servin', and I ain't had time to—*

Ah!

But, walking home, through the cold St. Paul night, a January night bluer than any uniform, Penny worried. What had she done? What would she do now? She had no skills, no prospects.

A problem for many post-bellum slaves, as Guy might say, these days.

5E) WHEN SHE GOT HOME, SHE HOPED GUY WOULDN'T SAY ANYTHING.

home /hoʊm/, n.

But he did.

"How was it, S.? The fields? The labor?" He lay there still, his definition sheets like bed sheets drawn nearly to his beautiful chin. "Same old, same old? The hot sun? Cruel Mistress Pen?"

She hated it when he called Pen "mistress." She closed her eyes at the word and saw Pen beside Guy in her own pitiable bed, a page of definition text discreetly placed over each ginormous breast. "She's not your mistress."

Guy laughed. "Oh, come on, cute little jealous

Slave, we've been over this, you know I only really love the help."

Penny's eyes were sore, as if from crying. She wanted to cry now, but didn't have the energy. *Cause when I'm givin' my all, when I'm servin' my Master, I ain't got time to...* Guy, she hated Guy. Hated that he would even joke about "Mistress Pen." Call her Slave—fine—Slave-kin, Slave-kitten—all fine, but never, never say mistress. No matter that this mistress was only ridiculous, blowsy Pen—no, because the mere suggestion that he wasn't her one, true—

And then she remembered. The one true truth. "She's not my mistress, either," Penny said. "Not anymore."

"Hunh?"

"I quit." She smiled. "After all, Mistress Pen was paying me, and it isn't exactly seemly for a little slave to get paid."

Guy looked at her. Oh, he was lovely. Their child would have his eyes, his nose, his dark mouth.

Guy looked at her. He looked and looked.

6a) HA!

ha! /hɑ!/, exclam. interj.

She'd finally discovered the solution! The final solution! Oh yes, no mercy, oh kill all the names!

Because call her a slave and she'd act like one. A
fish, a dish, a mutty cat. Oh, she'd act like them all,
oh yes! Glug-glug, smash, meow!

Ha!

And: oh, nefarious plan!

"I'm a house slave," she'd said, "not a field slave."
And here she was, a penthouse slave, lying all day
long on her unburdened back, her cheek zagged
with pillow marks, a jar of pitted cherries yawning
at her from the coffee table.

"Do you think you should get dressed?" Guy asked.

"Oh, yes, Master, oh, whatever you say, Master, oh, you just say the word, and get out the sackcloth, and just tell me what you'd have me wear today."

He sighed. He crossed his arms. "Sla-ave."

"Yes, Master?"

He threw his hands in the air, despairing, comic. Ha!

Ha.

But then it was the next day, and Guy was standing above her, a brown dress hooked on his finger and swaying in the January draft. The couch felt icy beneath her, the cushions blocky, her back stiff.

"Slave?"

"Mmm—wha—?"

The dress fluttered from his hand to her face, a mean brown bird.

"Why don't you put this on? I mean, look, I'm no stranger to, you know, 'depression.' Sometimes it helps to go through the motions. Trust me."

"Oh, okay, of course, Master. Of course I trust you." She struggled to right herself, her spine creaking. "But do you think you can help me? I'm not particularly educated, you see, and I'm not used to such garmentry. Zippers, and rayon, and if you could just find me some hemp with a hole for my head, that'd be much better."

Guy looked at her. Or so she thought. She could just make out his dim, cross-armed form through the cloth. Perhaps soon he would sit beside her, pull her close. Call her Penny, say he was sorry. But instead he said this, "Okay. I get it." He seemed to be looking into some mystical, sapiential distance. But what did he see? What did he *get*? Penny squinted through the cloth.

"You're right: that phrase is idiotic. I totally understand. I really do. I'll leave you alone."

6b) ha?

ha? /hɑʔ/, interrog. interj.

By Thursday, she needed to get up. To stretch her
fallow legs, to venture into the field. (The bathroom,
anyway.)

Fine. Maybe the final solution hadn't been so final. Maybe a less nefarious plan was in order. She'd
keep at this one, stooping and dragging her heels,
wearily moaning, "Ye-es, Master," at Guy's slightest
sound. But she'd seek alternative channels, as well.
Conventional channels.

She ordered a book titled *Loneliness!? What's
That?* She tried to hide it amid the couch cushions,
and behind the bondage magazine she'd—ha!—
ordered along with it. She didn't mind Guy see-

ing her—ha!—with *Slaves 'R Us*. But *Loneliness!? What's That?* would be her little secret.

Loneliness!? What's that?, the tome began. *Why, you'll have no idea by the end of your journey through these pages.*

Loneliness's cover was neon. The color of construction sites and Tang. It was difficult, therefore, to hide the book amid the cushions that now smelled of her wrists and inner elbows, salty and close. It was difficult even to hide the book behind glossy photos of blond-haired Flossy, whose fondness for wrought-iron cages and cast-iron muzzles had earned her "Miss February."

But Penny would do what it took. Once she and Guy (she and that vague guy who had been Guy) had been happy. And even now, in the jobless draft of January, Guy sequestered in the bedroom, it might still be possible to do as wise Dr. Trueheart—author not just of *Loneliness!? What's That?* but also of *Depression!? What's That?* and *Suicidal Ideation!? What's That?*—advised.

Loneliness is impossible for those of us who enjoy

our own company, Dr. T. wrote. *So nourish yourself!* Penny glanced up from the damp pages. The jar of cherries was empty now, and a jar of pimento-stuffed olives gawped—nearly empty—beside it. But was she, Penny, empty? Why no! She was full. Fed. Nourished. A little bit nauseated, even. Well past step one.

Onto number two!

Are you willing to speak to strangers? Penny looked out the window. At the blue-yellow day, at the empty street, the telephone lines hanging there like faceless smiles. Hello, Penny thought. She said it aloud. "Hello." It had been a good while since she'd spoken. "Hello, Street. Hello, Telephone Poles." She caught sight then, of her blurry self, in the panes. "Hello, Penny."

Did this count? After all, she looked like a stranger. Blurred and puddled. Casper-white. Her colorless hair a nest atop her birchy face.

The book was heavy. It tugged at her wrists. "What is it, Dr. T.?"

Don't be afraid to make the first move! T. answered.

Someone has to, right? Well, yes—Penny sat up, her vertebrae snapping into place, her skin staticky—and why not her? After all, stillness was the province of pretty girls—and Penny was not, etc., etc. She closed her eyes, saw herself corseted and gray-skinned, an old-movie slattern. She slouched in saloon light, rasped, "Hey there, pardner, anything I can getcha?" (Anything, Master? Anything?)

She shuddered at the vision, but why? Was it worse than this? The ants' footprints in the coffee table dust? The inside air that smelled like her own sick skin? She could give it a try, at least.

But first a few more words—a few more words would get her first-moving! Dr. T. was reassuring. *It's easy,* she wrote, *because the power is yours. At base, the first move is as simple as turning the nozzle in the shower. As lifting a hairbrush to your scalp. Give it a try. See? Did you need anyone's help? I offered the suggestion, but it was your hand lifting the brush handle, and your muscled arm lifting that hand!* Penny had lifted nothing, because the hairbrush was in the bedroom with Guy. She nodded anyway.

You feel good, right? Penny ceased nodding, but read on. *You feel useful. And you've learned a useful lesson. Because you've turned yourself from a sad sack, lying on a lumpy couch, to a useful, useful being! And you've done it all merely by changing the way you think. Which you will continue to do as you journey through these pages. Because, ultimately, if you change your thoughts of dependency, you will change yourself.*

Penny reread the line. *Change your thoughts of dependency.* Why not? Slaves were dependent, but Penny was not a slave. Penny was standing, moving toward Guy's door. No, it was her door, her bedroom, her bed with the broad art deco headboard, the one her mother had found at the Sunday flea market on 13th, the one her mother had died in.

(Oh, how to change when the scenery was always the same?)

Her hand was on the doorknob. White knuckles but no fear, and she closed her eyes—*change your thoughts*—saw herself supine on a striped towel. On white sand, white sun winding through her hair, lengthening it, lightening it. Her back sinking, stomach shrinking, legs stretching toward the sea as Guy fanned her with a giant leaf. His hand tight and white on the stem, and her own hand tight on the knob. She twisted it.

"Guy?"

"Slave?"

No. Her voice was husky, and she was moving forward. She was changed and unafraid, and she was saying his name again, "Guy."

"Good to see you're up, little Slavechen."

But she was not up. Her knees were buckling and she was falling to the mattress, crawling across the covers. She said it again, "Guy?"

"What is it? Do you want to get your old master a refill?" He held up his coffee cup, but she swatted at it.

"KLiKK?" Guy asked. "Is it you? Are you back, my Krazy Little Kitty-Kat? What have you done with Slavey?"

Oh, shut up. Penny closed her eyes, hoping for white sand, but there was nothing. No sand, just white, and so she batted the cup to the floor.

"What the—?" Guy cried.

"Shut up," she whispered. And she pressed her mouth to his.

Guy's lips were cold. They were inching away, two worms. "Mm. My papers." He spoke into Penny's chin.

"The cup was empty. They're fine."

Guy was squirming beneath her. "But—"

She cuffed his wrists with her hands. *Change your thoughts of dependency.* She pinned his wrists to the pillows. I am not a slave.

"My laptop!" His voice was loud and lovely, and he was pushing her off.

She looked at him. "Sorry." And then she was scrambling away, she was on her knees, on the floor. Stacking the unstacked stacks, saying, "See, it's fine, the cup was empty and these are fine, just, where should I put them?"

"Wait a second." Guy was kneeling too, bent over the laptop, his back to her. "Oh shit," he said.

"Sorry. But it's okay, I swear."

"Oh God," Guy answered. "Oh *Nigger!*"

She stacked. And she sighed and gasped, her breath huge and windy.

"Okay, it's okay," Guy said. "I wasn't sure I'd saved this part." Then, "S., what is it?"

"Nothing," she said. Nothing, nothing, I am not. But what had Dr. T. said? *The power is yours. Change your thoughts of dependency and you will change yourself.* It was hard to believe the wise doctor from here—on the floor—on her knees.

"Are you crying?" Guy asked. "Why are you crying?" Suddenly he was beside her, suddenly he was kneeling too.

"What is it?" she said.

He smiled. "That's what *I'm* asking."

"No. What is it about me? You call me these—"

And then words were spilling from her. Ridiculous globulous words, slavely and unslavely, but she couldn't stop. Though she was breaking the promises she'd made to her dear, dead mother. Admitting weakness and insecurity, and moving, moving. *Stay still! Keep still!* But her lips were wobbly, and her hands were trembling. They flapped about Guy's cheeks and ears and hair, they scurried under his shirt, flitted up and down his sides.

"What is it about me? Do you feel—?" She felt crazy, dizzy, feverish with illogic. This was Guy's logic, not hers, but the words still came. "Guilty? Because you're my master? I mean it really wouldn't be rape, I don't think. And there wouldn't be any miscegenation."

Guy laughed.

It was Guy's laughter, not hers—

But then it was hers, it was. She was laughing, flapping her hands with comic urgency, with seeming glee. "We could have children, Mast," she was barely able to say through her ha's. Her ha ha ha ha ha's! Ha ha! Ha! Ha? "I know you're Master and I'm Slave, but we'd find a way for you to—ha!—acknowledge your progeny!"

"Ha!" Guy, now. "Miscegenation! That's good. You really are a Krazy, Krazy Little Kitty!"

Ha ha!

Ha ha ha!!

Ha?

Guy frowned, though his eyes still smiled. Hunh... "Are you okay now? Are you sure?" He put his hand to her forehead. "You're kind of hot." At last! Victory! She wasn't disguuuuuussst-tiiinnnnnggg! She was hot! "Do you want to lie down?"

And she was back on the couch.

6c) HUNH.

hunh /hʌ/, interj.

Her plans had failed.

Every once in a while she'd try again, drag her heels along the dusty floor, sing field songs. (*Lord, I keep so busy servin'!*) She spoke at length of Thelma, her bff from the chain gang, but Guy just laughed. Laughed harder the further she took it, his lovely face hitching and notching with each absurd detail. Until Penny couldn't help but mirror him, become him. Until Penny couldn't help but laugh, too.

January passed, and February. In March, the St. Paul streets were paved with snow as gray as the sidewalks beneath. Penny stood at the window, eating cake, no plate, no fork. She watched the dull still street. Until she caught sight of something else

in the panes. Why, Penny. Hello there. Hello, Slave.
It had been so long since she'd looked in a real mirror. Suddenly, she was curious.

But when she got to the bedroom, Guy was
bending before the dressing table, staring at his
beveled face. He ran his index finger along his left
eyebrow.

"Hey there, Slavey T. Slavedoodle."

For once, she didn't laugh.

She must have frowned. Or stamped her foot.
Wept, perhaps. Keened.

"What's wrong?" he said.

"'Slavey T. Slavedoodle'?"

"You don't like that one?"

"That one? You think I like 'Slave'?"

"Wait, what's wrong with 'Slave'?" He looked
perplexed, then depressed. He smiled, tried widen-
ing his smile, but only looked pained and insane.
"After all, it comes from 'Slav.' I'm half Polish myself, as you know. Just 'taking back the language!'"

But she didn't laugh. No *ha*! No *ha*?

"Hunh?" she said.

"I don't know. I mean, sorry, sorry. It's just a meaningless hypocorism, anyway."

In the mirror, she saw Guy, his hands raised in uncertain defense, but she couldn't find herself. Maybe that had been Guy in the kitchen window as well, beauteous Guy, eating cake by the palmful. She walked toward the bed, slipped her feet into his vacant slippers. They were so soft she could barely feel them. And she could barely feel her feet as they slid across the room. Wasn't this better? She slipped beneath the sheets, gazed at the face blurred in the screen of the laptop. It was Guy, she was Guy, typing, deleting, seeking definition.

Hypocorism, n. 1. a name of endearment, a pet name 2. the use of such names.

Then some other Guy, or maybe just some guy, was beside her, kneeling on the bed, hovering in the screen. "The note was my idea."

The note: *Such words may not, in their original use, bear any resemblance in meaning to the meaning attached when used as a term of endearment, for example calling a paramour "pumpkin."*

"Pumpkin?" Penny asked. *"Pumpkin!"* She was yelling. "I should be so lucky!"

She was not Guy. He floated next to her in the white screen, they were both featureless in the blurry glare, but, still, she could see. Her plans had failed.

Every once in a while she'd try again, leap from floorboard to floorboard, one hand raised, crying, "I'm Spartacus... No, I'm Spartacus..." Or seek solace in texts. Not Dr. T. now, never Dr. T., with her fakey, carroty complexion, her fakey, failed counsel, but other texts, reliable texts, one line of text, at least, the very line that, only recently, had made her yell. *Such words may not, in their original use, bear any resemblance...*

But if she was not Slave, who was she?

She needed a mirror. To see. It had been weeks— no months!—since she'd looked. Finally, she found the full-length in the bathroom.

What she saw was this: hair, eyes, mouth. A bridesmaid's dress the color of a coffin's lining. She saw herself in a bridesmaid's dress and then Guy was there, behind her.

Vermilion. That was the word. There was no other word.

Guy was there, with his wide, kind grin, with the split mouth that said, *I totally get it*, even though he totally didn't.

Puffed sleeves, scooped neck. A black sash lashed around her ribs.

"You look pretty," Guy said.

Usage
AS IN:

Bridget Bridgman was getting married. Again.

Yes, Bridget Bridgman had been married ten years before, and Penny had been her bridesmaid then, too. She'd worn a different dress. They both had.

Penny's different dress had also been an indifferent dress: taupe, strapless, straight. Because, as Bridget Bridgman put it at the time, the wedding was to be *intimate,* and *tasteful,* just *good friends* and *muted colors.* Because Bridget, and Barney—her unfortunate ex, who looked like a kid at his first communion as he stood beside her on the altar—were poor.

Ten years hence, Bridget was rich. She wore snug suits, pinstripes fencing her in. And Penny wore a dress that was giant and vermilion.

Bridget called in February.

"Your maid of honor?" Penny said. "Are you sure?"

"You're my *oldest* friend," Bridget answered.

Penny was not young, but really?

They had lived on the same street as children.

They had played unsuitable games beneath Bridget's skirted dressing table (that necessity of romantic young womanhood, of childhood): markering tiny color-blocks onto the bands of Bridget's father's enormous, yellowing briefs; mime-smoking Bridget's mother's Veracruz Elegantés, then stubbing them out with socked feet. They played Bride too. It was Bridget's favorite. Unsurprising, because from the ages of two to thirteen Bridget was known as Bridey. So Bridey was bride and Penny was groom. But Penny hated pants, and, finally, Bridey let her be bridesmaid.

Imagine! Begging to be a bridesmaid.

She no longer begged. But she didn't say no. "Wow, Bridge." She sighed into the phone. "That really means a lot."

"I know!" Bridget said.

"Well," Penny said, "this is great."

"I know!"

"And you can meet Guy."

To which Bridget said, "I didn't realize it was so serious."

Bridget Bridgman was Penny's oldest friend. Bridget and Penny shared what oldest friends share: memories of soft chalk on hot pavement, of clammy tiny hands, of the sharp taste of snuck wine. Also: thinly concealed disdain, barely disguisable envy, and open suspicion.

Because, as a child, Penny was pretty. But a late bloomer. Bridget, on the other hand—Bridey— well, let's just say that boys were always dropping things, and saying, Bridey, can you pick that up? Boys never asked Penny to bend. Penny didn't even get her period yet, and they could smell it.

"Maybe you don't have a uterus," Bridey said. It was Sunday, and they were painting their nails on Bridey's bed. Bridey was content with no fewer than sixteen layers.

"I have a uterus," Penny answered.

"How do you know?"

"I know."

"How?"

Later, after countless pathetic and fantastic pro-testations—*I've had x-rays!*—Penny would write

81

it down. She'd keep a list, *Mean Things Bridey Has Said,* folded in squares beside the Hershey bar whitening in her bedside drawer. For all she knew, the list was still there. (Had Guy seen it? She didn't know whether the prospect excited or alarmed her, whether she wanted him to know everything or nothing...)

"I guess we're not that serious," Penny said into the phone.

"Well, yeah, but that doesn't mean it won't be good to meet him," Bridey answered. "We do have you down for a plus one."

u·ter·us /ˈyu tər əs/, n.

Plus one.

But Guy wouldn't want to come. "*Nigger* needs me!" he would say. "And sense 6b is so crucial!"

"I can't go," he'd say. "You can't make me, Slave." *You can't make me your slave.* But when she told him, he smiled. He'd always wanted to see Boston, where the wedding was, and it would be good for them to get away together.

"It would?" Penny asked.

"Yeah," Guy said. "I mean, um—" His eyes were suddenly filmy; he squinched them as if to squeeze away the grime. "Um," he said, "uh, ugh": a conjugation of discomfort. He shook his head. He quietly screamed. "Aaaggh! I mean, I'm not, like, insensate!"

But to speak of sensation seemed to make Guy—if not insensate—then insane. He tossed his head around hard, his shoulders slumping from the weight of whatever he couldn't shake away. His mouth opened, closed; his lips scurried from his nose to his chin and back, fleeing the words just behind them. "I'm," he said. "Uh, I mean—what was I saying?"

"You're not insensate?"

"Right!" Guy said, relieved. "Right," he repeated, unrelieved.

"It will be good for us to get away?"

"Right! Right. Um, my therapist always urges *me* to get 'out in the world' when things get, you know, really, like, *bad*. And I don't want to make you talk about it, I *totally, totally* get not wanting to talk about it, but, you know, I'm—worried. You're not happy, and—and—ah—and—aaagh—and—and—"

Penny had wanted this, of course: sympathy, sincerity. But she hadn't wanted *this*. "And—uh—um—erm—and—aeeghhaaa—em—mmm—and—" This stammering survey of suffering sounds, of every expression of unease. She would finish it. She would finish for him. "And," she offered, "it's not good business to have an unhappy slave?"

Guy's grateful laughter brought tears to both of their eyes.

So, in the coming weeks, Penny got her coffin lining altered, and Guy continued to redefine *sympathy* and *sincerity*, to draft new definitions of *concern*, *care*, *apology*, *alarm*.

At dinner, he reached across the green beans and

smoothed her hair. "Are you, you know, 'excited' about our upcoming 'escape'?"

Her mouth was full of beans. "Mmmph."

"I, um, I mean what I was trying to say the other day is I think it's, like, good, when you're dealing with, you know, a depression problem or whatever to 'look outside the self.'" He laughed. "Sorry, that's my therapist's stupid phrase. But, yeah, I mean it's really hard when there's no, I mean for me, I just work, I work and that helps, but for you—! I know it's been *especially* hard since—" Guy looked down at his plate. "Since, you know, you—you lost your spot in the field."

Penny was touched, for a moment, by his worry, cloaked though it was in this joke. "Are *you* excited?" she asked, a sudden, unaccustomed hope filling her.

"Of course." He reached across the beans again, squeezed her shoulder. His voice was kind, his hand a tender brand against her skin. "Just don't get any ideas when you see the Freedom Trail."

He winked significantly, and Penny's shoulder went cold.

No: there was no hope, and yet Guy kept speaking of it, his eyes blue with it, his hands upturned. I hope I don't look fat in my suit. And I hope it's not a buffet, and have you checked the weather, I mean, I hope it doesn't rain on poor Bridget, whom he'd never met, and who would never marry on a rainy Saturday, because, really, that just wasn't how life worked anymore. But still, Guy hoped for skies as clear and as blue as his eyes, and for allegiance to outmoded traditions—surprise, surprise!—because after all, it's funny when the bride throws the bouquet, and let's hope she has a garter, too, but let's also—please, please—hope they don't write their own vows, because original vows are unfailingly unoriginal. Pat and trite, corny and cheesy, because, let's face it, few people have any respect for the language these days, though maybe that will change when the third edition comes out, oh God, oh *Nigger*, oh Slave, let's hope.

Also, he hoped that she wouldn't miss her slave's quarters (the couch?), because good little slaves weren't accustomed to sleeping elsewhere. And he hoped she wouldn't be tricked and flattered by those liberal northerners, those broadminded easterners, with their narrow bedrooms and narrow shoes, the narrow strips of rock they called beaches. "They're bad news, Slavey," Guy cried. "They talk of freedom, but they're counting on your ignorance! Because you don't know how confining and lonely freedom really is!"

free·dom /ˈfri dəm/, n.

By the time they walked down the dreamy tunnel of the six-a.m. jetway, Penny felt, if not hopeful or free, then at least complacent. Amenable, biddable. Guy pushed her forward, and why resist? She was leaving horrible St. Paul, where the bitter streets all looked the same, and she was leaving the dull blur of these past months—so why not be bid-dable, beatable?

In fact, by the time she was lashed into seat 4F, Penny felt that she *had* been beaten. The suitcase she'd lugged from sidewalk to check-in to security, onto Gate 36B and seat 4F, had been so heavy with the enormous, sepulchral dress. Her right shoulder sagged and throbbed; the straps of her carry-on had branded her left.

"Excuse me, ma'am?"

She looked to her right, and felt suddenly water-logged. She was gazing through a plastic porthole, night swimming behind it. The sky was navy, land-ing lights switching, swishing like red and white fish.

"Ma'am?" Someone was speaking, not Guy, but some high, sweet, navy-suited bird. "Ma'am, will you please stow your carry-on?"

She hadn't heard anyone else speak in weeks. Just Guy. Who was elbowing her uninjured side.

"S.—your bag."

"Oh." She crammed it beneath her feet, glanced

up, seeking approval. She saw a lipsticked mouth, two circles of rouge like twin bruises. Penny felt she'd been beaten, but the bruised red cheeks were not her own. And the wide, frightened eyes were not Penny's either. They were green and brown and cluttered with—what? Concern? Affliction? Comprehension?

"You okay?" the red mouth asked. "Nervous?"

Penny nodded.

"You look like you could use a drink. You want a drink?" The red mouth waited, lips just parted.

Penny nodded obediently.

That was how it started. On the plane, Penny began to drink.

Why hadn't she thought of this earlier?

drink /drɪŋk/, v.

On the plane, Penny had two gin and tonics and a vodka on the rocks. The vodka was flavorless yet sweet, cool on her tongue, warm in her throat. She swallowed it and tasted tarnished silver, an unpolished kitchen knife scraping her larynx. The gin was different. Penny swallowed, and her mouth—delighted just moments ago, fizzy with tonic—felt stung. Her stung tongue grew peppery and heavy and furred. Her vision zagged. There was the window, a fuzzy aquarium swimming with stars. But, no, that was Guy's open mouth, Guy's black maw, spittle coming with each snore, silver flecks starring the air. Airplane air, in need of changing, like water in a fishbowl. Her head bobbed. Her lids sunk and rose, buoyed by fizz that seemed, again, to travel up instead of down her throat, up and through her nose. The fizz effervesced behind her eyes, and was gone. Up down. Blink blink. Black white. She could see everything and nothing. Guy's mouth, like a lens, a binoculared circle, his teeth huge. She could count his taste buds. One, seventeen, forty-six. But she couldn't count, her eyes were closed. She couldn't see anything at all.

That was gin. Vodka was necessary, then, to scrape her out, to cleanse and restore her.

scrape out /skreɪp aʊt/, v. phr.

The airport was one giant flash bulb. They disembarked unsteadily into the glare, Guy's hand at her elbow, his mouth a machine of sighs. "Come on," he said, his voice as scraped-out as her throat, "let's get some food into you."

But Penny didn't open the menu. When the waitress came, yellow fish bobbing across her apron strings, suspending themselves on her name tag, whispering PAM T., Penny nodded toward the bar. "Are you serving?"

Pam understood. "Bloody Mary?" she asked, grinning. Pam was Penny's soulmate.

"Pancakes," Guy said. He didn't say anything else.

Not until he'd beaten his pancakes into submission. Not until he'd stared for six whole minutes at his lovely reflection—in the silver napkin dispenser, in his serrated grapefruit spoon, in each of his perfectly round, ridged fingernails. Not until he had twisted his straw into a noose.

Then he said, "Look."

But Penny couldn't focus. Anyway, what she saw did not make sense. There was her drink, the sweating glass, the pallid celery stick, the ice cubes dotted with pepper—translucent dice—but where was the drink—the tomato juice, the vodka? She didn't remember drinking it. Her eyes zoomed in on a cocktail onion. She could see each of its white veins—one, eighteen, forty—she could see the overhead fixture, reflected in precise miniature, in the onion's burnished skin.

"Look," Guy said again. He went on, though she didn't obey. "I—I mean. Ugh. Why are you making me do this?" He sighed. He tried. "Look," he repeated, but try as she might, Penny couldn't. Her eye had become a cocktail onion, and the world had grown skin.

"I know things have been fucked up with us. I know I'm fucked up. I know I have trouble with, you know, the 'emotional' side of, ugh—see, that's the thing. It's not the emotions, I mean maybe it is a little, but mostly it's not, it's just the *language*."

Guy's voice came from far away. She was an onion now, her ears filled with loam.

"Don't you get that?" he continued, his voice as clogged as her ears. "I thought you got it. It's not, like, *love*, it's just the word *love*. And it's like, I *do* want you to feel better, I really do, but I don't want to say something dumb like, 'Duh, I hope you feel better—'"

Penny's neck snapped.

Her head lifted, pulled by some sudden filament. She thought she heard something crack or tear—roots, a sheet—a sheet of ice blocking frozen soil. She could see again. She could see Guy perfectly. She looked him straight in the eyes.

"Guy," Penny said. Not Master, not Itty-Bitty-Kitty-Keeper—"Guy. I have never felt better in my life."

bet·ter /ˈbɛt ər/, adj.

That was the last thing Penny said to Guy. The last full sentence, anyway. She spoke a word here and there in the wonderful hotel, where daffodils leaned sympathetically from the nightstand, where the open windows were tall as doors, but nothing more. She had no use for Guy in this new world, where she was not a slave, where polished sea-stones gleamed on the coffee table. By the time they arrived at the wedding, Penny wasn't speaking to Guy at all. He acted angry ("Really, *really*? This is really how you want to play it?"), but she could tell he was relieved. He didn't stammer. His consonants were crisp, his vowels ungarbled, and Penny could tell her silence was a kindness.

So Penny was kind. She didn't speak to Guy at the ceremony, as she stood, regal and ghoulish, on the altar. And at the reception, she was utterly una-ware of Guy's whereabouts, of his staggering, lonely trips to the bar, of the awkward witticisms he tried on strangers. ("Have you heard the one about the cannibals and the clowns"?) She was unaware of the hors d'oeuvres he lifted from greasy doilies. She was unaware of his Jacuzzi eyes and clamshell finger-nails. Because at the reception, Penny had Bridey. And she had a sweating glass of white, always—miraculously—full.

Bridey clung to Penny's vermilion arm. "Did I look insane?"

"Don't be insane!" Penny answered.

They laughed.

"I thought I was going to throw up."

"An old pro like you?"

Penny could feel Bridey's breathy laugh against her cheek. It was strange at first—Bridey's proximity. That's Guy's cheek, Penny caught herself thinking. That's Master's! Bridey's breath smelled of cucumbers and pepper and dried petals. They walked past a mirrored wall, Bridey clutching Penny's elbow, and Penny spied another petal, in her cheek. She was purple, blooming. Bridey leaned in. "Look at us," she said.

And then, in their drunk closeness, in the inch of space between them and the mirror, in the smells of seven-dollar chardonnay and laundered satin, all that had been between them flew away. Disdain, envy, suspicion. They clung together.

"You look beautiful," Penny said.

"Come on," Bridey said to Penny. "Let's find a

waiter. Let's find another drink." Her dress announced itself as they moved among the guests, swishing, sssing. It caught the light of the hotel chandelier, and snipped and flashed like a thousand tiny scissors—moving, closing—opening the hotel air so that Penny and Bridey could move through it.

"Oh, Bridey," Penny said, "your dress is made of scissors."

Bridey laughed. "You are wasted!"

Guests approached. They floated forward on clouds of drugstore perfume and bordelaise and whiskey. They leaned into Bridey, whispering congratulations. They mouthed Penny's word, *beautiful*. Their voices were wispy, their grips light. Penny scrunched her nose, clung to Bridey's arm, even as the guests came close. Even as they rotated their faces toward her. "You must be proud."

Penny gulped her wine. "Mm-hm. And her dress is made of scissors."

A blue-jawed man looked at her quizzically.

Bridey laughed. "Ben, have you met my maid of

honor? Penny?"

Ben shook his blue head.

A woman leaned in. Her face was crumpled paper, her hair was full of flowers. Her eyelids moved slowly along her eye-whites, dishrags along porcelain. "You must be so happy for our Bridget."

"Of course," Penny said. "I would never *ever* want to get married myself. But, I mean, I know Bridge is happy. And of course I'm happy for her because Bridge is so, so happy!"

But was Bridey happy? In the church, Penny had stared at her friend across the altar, willing her to look back. But Bridey's eyes were fixed on Brent, the tall, balding groom, the tall, balding software engineer. His chirpy voice and sequestered millions usually filled Bridey with shivery pleasure, though in the church she'd seemed stricken and stiff. Maybe she needed a drink. Penny certainly did. Soon, she kept telling herself. Soon there would be champagne on the lawn as the photographer snapped pictures, as she and Bridey and the others clutched each other formally. And now that was forever ago, the sun was setting through the windows, and Bridey's voice rang against the ceiling, unnaturally loud. "Be nice, Pen. Be polite."

And Bridey's voice rang across years, "Be nice to me. Why can't you just be nice to me?" Bridey stood weeping at the foot of Penny's bed. They were sixteen. Penny had taken up with the first of her mean men, and Bridey had come crying into her bedroom, after weeks of restraint. Her voice was terrible, enormous, gluey with tears. "Why can't you be nice? You're so nice to him, you do anything he says. But he won't be around forever. Not like me." She had brought Penny a pie, a silver disc filled with chocolate Jell-O and Cool Whip. She balanced it between her ribs and one hand. Penny lay on the bed, concentrating on her own face, calming each feature in turn. Relax your brows, she thought. ("Keep still," her mother had said.) She closed her eyes, expunged the lines from her brow, thinned her nose, parted her lips, breathed out and in, never looking at Bridey.

"Be nice," Bridey said again.

"You know," Penny had answered, "I don't really like chocolate."

"Be polite," Bridey was whispering now, hissing.

"He's not even nice to you," Bridey had wailed. "Not the way I am."

"You're right," Penny answered, sinking her nails into Bridey's satin arm.

"Ouch," Bridey said. Then, whispering again, "It's no big deal, Penny. I don't particularly care for the old lady myself. She is Brent's godmother though, so, you know, no need to offend."

"But you're right," Penny repeated. "You're right. He's not nice to me. He acts like he's being nice, but he's not. It's not nice to call someone those things."

Bridey's mouth was close. It was huge and pink, a magnified sea plant. It was all Penny could see. And Bridey's voice was all Penny could hear. It was low, slow. Are. You. All. Right. Penny took a breath. The air tasted sharp. But smooth, too. Grapefruit, with a butterscotch finish, and where was her wine? She felt the lip of the glass against her own lip. She was swallowing and speaking at once. "He seems nice, but..."

"Are you all right, Penny? I told you it's not a big deal. Is everything okay?"

If Penny concentrated, she could make Bridey's blurry face distinct. She knew it so well, as well as her own, better than Guy's. "You're right," Penny whispered. "He's not nice like you."

"Come with me," Bridey answered. "Let's talk."

talk /tɔk/, v.

In the corridor outside the ballroom, Bridey's face was bright. "He calls you what?"

Penny examined each feature. The large swirly eyes. The tiny nose, just turned up. Bridey had always hated it. As a child, she'd refused to answer to her full name because Angus Huntington had torqued and mangled it, chasing her beneath the slides, calling, "Pidget, Piglet!" But looking at it now, Penny loved Bridey's nose. Not the way she had before, luxuriating in its flaw, in the trick it played on Bridey's otherwise even face. Now she loved it because it was small and sly, mischievous in its reversal, its refusal to straighten. Penny smiled. "You're so pretty."

"Here, why don't you have a little more water?"

That was Brent, Bridey's second husband—imagine: two husbands!—some people had all the luck. But Penny looked at Bridey's twitching mouth. She was trying not to smile, Penny knew, but she couldn't believe what she'd just heard. Slave! Guy called Penny Slave!

"Do you think it's maybe, like, a sexual thing? Like he's trying to hint that he's interested in, I don't know, dominating you or something?" Bridey's wedding dress rustled. Penny imagined a thousand birds beneath, their twitters barely stifled by satin and crinoline, their wings ruffling.

"Do you think that's what it is?" This was Moira, Penny's underling, Bridey's maid of dishonor.

"Oh, no." Penny smiled. "No! We don't even have sex!"

Brent coughed.

"Jesus, honey." Bridey had lipstick on her perfect teeth.

Braces, Penny thought. If only I'd had braces, Mom, then maybe this wouldn't be happening.

"Je-sus," Bridey repeated, giving equal emphasis to each syllable. "What are you even doing with him?"

Someone giggled. Penny ran her eyes quickly over each face. Bridey, her smeared teeth. Brent was blushing but grinning. And there was Moira, her hand at her mouth. Moira, who'd slumped this morning under her sarcophagus of a dress, whose mouth had been thin and dark as an old scab, was now unable to contain her hilarity. Penny smiled. She had made these strangers happy. They looked as happy as Guy when she stooped and dragged her feet, pantomiming chains at her wrist, mouthing,

"Water, water." Give me water, I'm thirsty.

"Not ever?" Moira asked. Nodding, urging her on.

"Not ever! And I'm thirsty."

Her audience laughed. But Penny *was* thirsty. She lifted her wineglass, drained it. Raised her wrist, and attempted a flamenco snap. "Garçon?" Her audience laughed again.

And Penny laughed as a waiter half her age, acne like five-o'-clock shadow on his chin, stooped to fill her glass. She managed to laugh even as she took her first sip, her eyes closed, the hotel light coming pink through her lids. Oh, this was life, a new life. Music throbbed in the papered wall. The lyrics were loud, blurred, words of love stopped and confused, turned to yowls, to fighting. And Penny had turned to someone new. The wine was on her tongue, it was in her bitten, living skin, and she was new, a gal's gal, snickering, radiant. Her mother had urged on her a type she could never master (ugh: *master*), someone languid and entrancing, supine on a divan, posed, poised. The dignified girl who smiles slowly, whose skin is cold as an oyster's shell. But Penny was free now. Her mother was dead, and Guy was somewhere behind the wall, in the yowling music, and Penny was hilarious and alive, an audience at her feet, a delicate glass in her clumsy hand.

Hello my name is Plain Penny, I have never been pretty!

She hitched her heavy skirts up. So what if her audience saw the runs in her hose, her stubby dangling shoes, they'd still listen. Bridey and Brent's very wedding, and yet they were out here in the hall with her, rapt at her feet, as she spoke her mean, sad, amusing truths. They shook their heads, shocked, delighted. Poor Penny, they thought. They couldn't resist her.

Hel-lo-my *name*-is-Plain *Pen-ny, I-have nev*-er-been *pret*-ty!!

Bridey couldn't resist her. Indeed, Bridey was grabbing her, holding on. "Oh my God," she said, "did you hear that?" Yes, Bridey's hands were talons on Penny's ankles. "Don't Stop Believin'!" She pointed toward the ballroom. "That's the signal. Penny, it's toasts after this."

Then Bridey was pulling Penny—"Let's go, we've got to hurry!"—and Brent had taken her wineglass, replaced it with a half-carafe of water. "Drink," he said.

"Penny, are you going to be okay for this?" Bridey was asking. "Are you going to be okay? Because Moira can fill in…"

Penny didn't answer. It was hard to make out Bridey's words in all the bustle and fluster and flutter. They were huddled together still—Moira, Brent, Bridey, Penny—but they were moving too, through the giant doors of the ballroom, out and onto the floor. The yowls turned to words— "Some will win, some will lose, Some were born to sing the blues—" and Bridey's satin flapped and sang, and Moira was all Penny could see. Moira's black curls like oxidized springs, Moira, leading Penny by the hand. Then she was at Penny's ear, whispering.

"Good luck," she said. "I'm glad it's not me but I know you'll do great." She laughed.

"Don't stop believin'," someone was saying,

"hold on to that feelin'."

Penny nodded. Yes, hold on—the bitten veins, the wine cutting her throat, laughter scratching her ears. And then another voice interrupting, echoey and huge: "And now the maid of honor, Penelope Smith, will toast the bride and groom."

Penny was atop the bandstand, a microphone heavy in her hand.

"Wait," someone shouted from the crowd.

Penny's heart wheeled.

"Wait!" A man's voice—Guy's? Where was he? She scanned the crowd: their flushed, upturned faces, their eyeglasses like tiny mirrors—she could see herself, reflected, refracted, there and in their champagne glasses, held aloft and expectant. Was he out there? She imagined him parting the crowd, running to her across the parquet. "Wait!" he would say. "I didn't mean it. You're not a slave. I love you!"

Or: "Get down from there, Slavey. You're not up for auction."

But another man was before her, standing on

his tiptoes just below the bandstand, his nose level with her knees. He wore red suspenders, a bowtie. He lifted his arm.

Was it him, finally? Her one true love? She hadn't anticipated suspenders, but she'd made mistakes before.

"Penelope," the man scolded, "you can't toast without a proper drink!"

And he took the half-carafe of water—which, comically, she still held—replaced it with a flute of champagne, that necessary component of romantic young womanhood, though Penny was no longer young.

She lifted it gratefully. Bent her neck to take a drink.

"Wait," someone else cried, "you have to toast first!" Someone else laughed. Someone else cleared his throat, as if to suggest to Penny a proper means of commencement. The audience was so helpful tonight! Penny smiled, suddenly enjoying their augmentation. Why, moments ago, it had just been Moira, Brent, and good old Bridey, but now, generously, her friends had copied themselves, populating the entire floor. Penny looked at them, all these Moiras, Brideys, Brents, at their eager slanting grins.

"Well," Penny said, and the Moiras waited. The Brents waited, delighted, chuckling. The Brideys chuckled too, confident of imminent hilarity.

"Rules were made to be broken!" Penny lifted the flute to her lips, gulped the champagne. "Can anyone offer me another?"

To be sure: laughter all around. Even a few appreciative gasps. The champagne crowded Penny's throat and chest. Good old Suspenders—a soulmate just like Pam—was handing her another. Penny gazed lovingly at him as she bent to take it, at his cheeks, waxy and red as apples on display, at the fizzy sparkle of his eyes. He wouldn't remember any of this tomorrow.

She raised her second glass, and upended it, guzzling.

More gasps. Followed by new varieties of laughter: hehs replacing hars, enunciated hos replacing hahs, murmured words interrupting all the while.

"Hey!" someone called. Guy? No, Brent. The original Brent. "Save some for the fish!"

The audience laughed louder, harder, approving and thankful.

But Penny would go him one better. "Hey," she chirped back. "Hey, hey," she sang, "like you can't spare the pesetas!" *Pesetas*? Why had she said *pesetas*? She felt her feet wobble in the stumpy velvet shoes—dyed vermilion to match her inane costume, not that you could see them under all that funereal fabric. *Pesetas.* A misstep, possibly. But no! Laughter, more laughter, laughter all around. Brent laughed loudest, between cries of "Touché!" Though his face had taken on a strange green-gray cast.

"En garde!" Penny replied. "But just one more glass, please. For real this time."

Suspenders gave her another, and she squeezed his hand.

She raised the flute, but there was no need to guzzle. She could feel Glass Number Two's faint sparkle within her fingers. "A toast," she cried, "to Bridget and Brent, of course, for having such wonderfully alliterative names."

Guy would appreciate that. Anyone with respect for the language would.

She lowered Glass Three, pressed it to her chest. The bubbles inside turned, in her mind, to little, glittering hearts, throbbing in gold time with her own. She pressed the grille of the microphone to her lips. "You know," she started, and already they were laughing, elated by nervous expectance. Penny knew their pleasure would be even greater if she made them wait, so she lifted the glass again, and took a modest half-sip.

"You know, I've known the bride—the bride, the Bridey—Bridget. I've known Bridget for as long as I've known myself. And I can't tell you how happy I am to see her happy now.

…Can't tell you because I'm *not* happy! No, no, kidding, kidding, I'm happy, we're all happy. …Except Brent! But seriously, kidding. And Bridge is so happy. And in love." Penny hiccupped. Laughter hiccupped beneath her. "Some of us never find love."

She raised her eyes to the domed plaster, and suddenly she was inside the wedding cake. The ceiling was buttercream. It arched and dropped in dollops and curlicues, the chandeliers drooping and twirling and throwing spoonfuls of light across the walls, until the plaster glittered like fondant. Penny lifted her glass, then lifted her other arm. Ta-da! The girl filling the cake. Doesn't matter if she's pretty. So long as she surprises. So long as she puts on a show.

She would bring the house down. The sweet walls would crumble.

Hĕllŏ mў̆ / nāme ĭs plăin / Pēnnȳ / Ī hāve / nĕvĕr bĕen / prēttў̆!!!

"Some of us never find love! Some of us never know what it is to gaze deep into the eyes of our soulmate! I mean, look, look, right now, at the way Brenty and Bride, I mean Bridey and Brent, gaze at each other!"

Although Brenty and Bride were gazing at Penny, if gazing was even the word. Their four eyes were hard, their mouths inch-long lines.

"Some of us never find love," Penny said, looking away from them, up at the decadent ceiling. "I, for example, came here with my own 'true love.' Where are you, Guy? Guy? I know he's here somewhere!"

A few timid twitters from the crowd.

"I know, right? Who could resist this?" Penny gestured at her vermilion death-costume, stumbled slightly in her velveteen shoes. "Ha! Ha ha! Go ahead, laugh, please! But, anyway, Guy, where are you?"

She raised a flat hand to shade her eyes, pretended to scan the crowd. Make them wait. That's what her mother had said.

"Oh, that's right!" Penny slapped her forehead. "Master? Master, are you out there? See, I call him Master. Never Guy. And you know what he calls me?"

Then Penny saw his face. It was fluttering on her inner eyelids, handsome as ever, with its straight nose, its red mouth, its uncommon, nearly aberrant symmetry. He flashed a smile and nodded. That's right! Say it! His mouth tugged up at the corners, his nose scrunched one bit, then another. He was smiling, wide then wider, his face tugged up and out in measured escalations of happiness.

So Penny did as she was told. She slumped her back and dropped the hand holding the glass, as if the delicate flute were a shackle. Her knees knocked together. She shuffled wearily, as if she were being dragged stage-left by invisible chains.

"You know what he calls me?" she repeated, miming her role as she spoke. "Guy?"

She blinked and there he was. She blinked, then kept her eyes closed, and there he was, nodding, bending his neck and hunching his shoulders, just as she did. He was unconsciously acting out the insulting role he'd assigned her, his grin reversing itself, though his eyes still smiled, their crinkly corners unmaking his face's perfection. She lived for this. For the hitches and notches in his too-smooth face, for the way she could turn him into her—turn him to Penny, make his face a new face—a girl's face, mirror-plain, cluttered with sadness and happiness and penury.

He nodded. Yes, he mouthed, I call you my most wondrous, loveable, funny, cute, cuddly, little—

"Slave," Penny said. "Slave."

Her voice rang across the ballroom, echoing against the frosted walls.

She opened her eyes. Hundreds of Moiras and Brideys and Brents crowded below, watching her, their mouths open, opening, just about to laugh. No Guy, but hundreds of Moiras, Brideys, Brents, waiting, wanting only to laugh. Why didn't they? What else did she have to say? Did they want her to put on her slave show, sing a work-ditty or two? She could segue seamlessly enough back to Bridey and Brent, she supposed, Bridey first. Bridey, her first master, her childhood mistress, who'd had Penny sing that other slave song, the wedding march. Bridey had stepped slowly down the white aisle of her winter walkway, her unringed hands clasping a bouquet of brittle twigs, as Penny obediently crooned, "Dum, dum dee dum, Dum, dum dee dum." Penny never sang the words, just *dum, dum, dum, dumb, dumb*—

She was singing now, she realized. "Dumb, dumb, dumb." She'd always loved the feel of a microphone in her hand, its cool, metallic heat, its weightless heft—

But this microphone's weightlessness was unnatural. Her right hand was empty. Her left held an empty flute. Yes: Penny looked from left to right to left to—right: no microphone, just Moira. Moira's face was done up like a mime's, and she was silent, her mouth in a twist as she tugged at—oh yes—not her vermilion skirts, but the microphone's cord— she was lifting it to her mouth, clearing her throat. "Excuse—"

"Wait," Penny said. "I was just about done."

But Moira wouldn't look at her. So Penny looked at the crowd, seeking some other, better Moira. "I was just about done," she repeated, catching a man's eye. Just another Brent? Or was it—could it really be—Guy?

He was nodding.

Penny blinked. The maybe-Guy blurred and smeared. He was a smudge. But her smudge! Maybe? "I'm just about done," she yelled. "Don't worry! I was just about done!"

The man, the guy, her smudge, took shape. And Penny could see each feature of his face in crystalline, spun-sugar detail. The small, black eyes, close-set above the snub of a nose. That nose, which was distinctly, definitely unlovely—porcine even. Yet he nodded. Penny could see the fat lips moving slowly, forming definite, definable words.

Yes, he said, you are done.

Moira and Penny stumbled from the bandstand. There was a cough here, a sigh there, and soon enough the room was a chorus of exhalations, slow sips, cleared throats. But no one spoke.

Penny had said enough.

au·di·ence /ˈɔ di əns/, n.

Later, Bridey talked: "Jesus, Penny, I know things aren't going well for you, and I'm worried about you, really, but Jesus, Jesus God: at my wedding!?"

Penny looked up. A white plastic sky, light spots spinning. Where were they? She tipped her head and there was Bridey, her skirts filled with songbirds. She was leaning against something—a white pedestal, a large white bowl, a swirly sound rushing from it. A birdbath for the birds beneath her dress. Her hems floated above the ground, which was green and slick, cut into tiny squares. Something blurred and swirled in Penny's stomach. She turned again, pressed her cheek to something cold.

Moira's hands were in Penny's hair. "Come on," she said. "Just pull the trigger."

And then Bridey was speaking, she was weirdly loud, she wouldn't stop. Penny could feel Bridey's voice move into her ear, step along her lobe, then stick minute stilettos into her red inner skin. Penny could see her too, plopping onto an eardrum in her flying cloud of a dress. Beneath her, the eardrum resembled a Christmas ornament. It was a white cylinder, gilded rope x-ing its sides, two gold sticks fastened in another x. Bridey sighed, and her roaring breath filled Penny. "At my wedding!" she cried.

Penny shook her head, but Bridey wouldn't get out. *At my wedding! At my wedding! At my wedding! Jesus! Jesus! Jesus!*

"Jesus," Penny echoed. She was inside the birdbath now, gazing at her blurry face in the swirling water. "It's not like you can't just have another one!" Really—Penny thought, blinking trills into the dark water, watching her own face twirl down a wide white hole—some people had all the luck.

hole /hoʊl/, n.

Penny woke in the hotel. The lamps were on, but the sky outside was dark. The high windows had turned to black tiles. Penny sat up, feeling as if she was hitting her head against something soft and close, her ears filled with muffled thuds. Was Bridey inside still? Had she replaced her stilettos with slippers? Was she sprawled along Penny's ear canal in her expensive honeymoon lingerie?

Penny looked at the floor, where the sheets lay humped and tangled. Penny's vermilion dress sprawled beside them, staining the carpet like a slain woman. Or like vomit. Which was everywhere. Penny couldn't see it, but she could smell it, acrid on her pillow, in her hair, on her hands, which clawed the quilted bedpad.

There was a gash in one of her knuckles. She wore nothing but her underwear.

Penny, lover of beautiful words and beautiful songs and beautiful stories, squeezed her eyes shut. The story here was simple. Someone—Bridey? Brent, oh please not Brent? Probably Moira, but could Moira have handled it herself? Maybe Guy had helped her? But no. He would be here still. He would be here.

He wasn't here.

Someone, Moira probably, had borne her away from the wedding cake ballroom, from the butter-cream ceiling, from the birdbath bathroom. Someone had borne her here, helped her out of her death costume. Stripped the sheets once Penny had soiled them. Arranged her feet below the scratchy blanket that had, just that morning, been folded neatly in the closet.

Penny stood. The room twirled. Music tripped through the carpet as she stumbled across it, a jazz waltz, and the room twirled again in response. The black squares of window rearranged themselves, box-stepping, promenading. At her touch, the panes froze. The world behind them twirled instead, planes falling and rising. Penny could just make out the lights on the wings and tails, lifting, blinking. She fixed her eyes on one light, one shrunken distant heart, beating, beating. She couldn't see the attached plane, but it was there, she knew, full of trapped faces, pressing noses and cheeks to their own windows. Penny pressed hers harder against the hotel glass, trying to make out the distant plane's body, the bodies inside. But she couldn't see anything, couldn't see anyone, not Guy, who was on that plane probably, flying away from her, to St. Paul, where he would climb into a taxi, where he would turn to a yellow blur in the black night, speeding to the penthouse to retrieve his things.

Penny could feel the champagne in her still, whirlpooling in her stomach, rising in her throat. Champagne. What a mistake. In her mind, Guy nodded, repeating after her, "A mistake." He stalked through the St. Paul penthouse, grabbing books, sweaters, stuffing them into a duffle bag. It had been a mistake, he meant, to settle so easily into Penny's penthouse, to settle so quickly into Penny's life, to settle for Penny.

"Wait—" He turned, lifting his face from the scattered piles. "I didn't 'settle' for you. You understood my playfulness, played along. I thought you understood it, I thought you had respect for—" He stopped, shook his head.

He was right to shake it. Penny wasn't playful but pliable. She wasn't funny or fun, just functional. The function of whatever mean man—

"I'm not mean!" Guy cried, in her mind. His face was red, and he waved his papers emphatically. "Jesus, Slave—Penny—oh, whoever, whatever, I never thought I'd say this, but they're just words!"

He was wrong. Call her slave and she turned to one. Even now, in the empty hotel room—the real live Guy thousands of miles above her and blacked out by night—Penny stooped and moaned. Call her a slave and she'd turn to one. She dragged her feet across the carpet, away from the window.

Dragged her weary self to the mattress, to the lumped bedpad.

"Wait—" Guy cried, but his voice was miles away, soft as the hum of invisible planes. "Wait, you're making a mistake." But other sounds filled Penny. She could hear Bridey between her ears, heeled feet like snare-sticks on her eardrum. "At my wedding," Bridey said. And Penny could hear her other mistakes, she could see them in the room with her. Pesetas jangled in the hanging lamp, then twirled through the air, jingling like the laughter that had refused to follow Penny's toast. Her vermilion dress stood up and brushed itself off, disgusted at the thought of that toast. It waltzed to the dark window, flung itself through. "At my wedding," Bridey said. "Jesus God: at my wedding." Guy tried to interrupt, but his voice was so weak, so muddled in the cluttered room.

And in the morning, every voice was quiet. No one spoke to Penny as she brushed her throbbing, vomit-caked teeth, pulled on her clothes. Guy was gone, her nocturnal suspicion confirmed. He'd left before whoever-it-was had borne her back, stripped her, stripped the bed, tucked her in. His suitcase was missing.

One of the clouds in the giant window was suitcase-shaped, though, a bloated rectangle, packed too tight. A wispy handle wavered atop it, on the verge of breaking. "Look at that," Penny said. But no one answered.

Obsolescence

Not Guy, who sat in the aisle seat—28B—his legs stretched beneath a blue blanket.

"Guy?" Penny stood in the aisle.

No, he didn't answer, just folded his blanketed legs at the knees, making space for her to step around him.

But through the window other people spoke. Other men. A tall man with a round face like an orange, his tanned skin a wrinkled peel, a hardhat on his head. His mouth opened in his beard. His arms wagged and wheeled, waving another man, who dragged a pulley piled with suitcases, toward the plane.

Penny turned from the window. "Guy?"

He didn't answer.

Outside, the orange man spoke, his red mouth opening new directives into his beard. "Wait," Penny thought she saw him say. But then the plane was moving, lifting. The earth became whirling quicksand—all of it—the lit, black runways, the airport, which had been flat as a playing card moments ago, the navy blue Atlantic—all sucked down and away, whirling into an invisible drain, into obsolescence. They'd escaped. They were moving away from it, away from Boston, from the present and recent past, the toast, the debut of Slave, back to before, to St. Paul. But even as the plane rose, and as the world recoiled, Penny felt stuck.

She felt the stuck stillness of the air. She inhaled in gulps, but felt as if she couldn't breathe, and, when she spoke, the words seemed to bounce back into her mouth.

"Guy?"

"Guy?"

"Master?"

Call her slave and she'd turn to one. But now, he wasn't calling her anything.

So Penny slept. Closed her eyes, and saw nothing but Bridey finally, Bridey at sixteen, lids painted robin's-egg blue. She was sixteen but she wore her wedding dress.

"Listen," she said. "You should listen because I know you. I know *you*." But then she wasn't Bridey. She was Penny's mother, all got up in Bridey's cloud of a gown.

"It doesn't matter anymore," her mother said. "It doesn't matter." Her skin was transparent. "Oh look at me. Just look at me." Her eyes were larger than they'd been in life, stuck open by surprise.

Penny woke above Michigan. Guy was asleep.

"Guy?" she whispered.

He pulled the blanket up. Shifted on his shoulder toward her. "Mm?" His were eyes still closed.

"Guy?" But she didn't know how to ask the question—the syntax kept shifting, the words do-si-doing, linking arms, swishing, switching.

What is going to become of us?

What are we going to become?

He spoke eventually. The plane moved west, and his elbow slipped on the armrest, touching hers.

He looked her in the eyes as if he knew her, said, "Are you fucking serious? I'm not talking about this on the *plane*. You think you could wait until we're alone? Jesus Christ. Until we're home?"

So. They would be going home together, in one blurry yellow cab, to the inevitable penthouse. But like Penny's mother said: it didn't matter anymore.

When they were thirty-six thousand feet above Wisconsin, the stewardess finally came around. "Ma'am," she said. "You want something to drink?"

Penny ordered a Bloody Mary, not looking at Guy. She took the cool plastic cup from the waitress, and turned from whatever expression Guy wore, to the window. She pressed the plastic to her lips and took a peppery sip. Pressed her forehead to the plastic oval opening like a mouth in the side of the plane.

Lights flashed below. Two, then four, green, yellow, red. What time was it? Penny lifted the cup to her mouth, but found it empty. Ice chips knocked her teeth. The distant lights persisted. Blue, green, green, blue. Small, clustered, a swarm. Penny lifted the cup again—she would chew the peppery ice chips—but found only her empty hand. The lights were white, then yellow. It was as if the stars had sunk from the heavens, and were constellating now, below the plane. Or maybe the plane itself had risen up, up, far enough above the earth to lap the least hearty stars.

"We're over Madison now," the Captain announced. So it was only Wisconsin. There was a famous air show in Wisconsin, Penny knew. The AirVenture, in Oshkosh. The father she'd never known had gone every year. So maybe those were the lights of planes. Other planes filled with other women and men, performing their dangerous tricks. The loopy rises and falls, the planes zooming and hurrying, propellers beating like mad, reckless hearts. Penny imagined the spectators below. Her father in a brown suit, holding a sandwich in one hand, brisket on rye. He takes a bite, then drops it. The noise is too loud, see? And he's no better than the rest of them, the crying children, the women in their sad loud dresses, all of them pushing their hands against their ears.

Penny's plane was quiet. Its hum was constant, but polite: the hum of an old desk lamp or a heater. The hum of some household appliance, some machine designed to protect her from the world, to abet her delusions. Don't worry, Penny, it isn't cold out there. It isn't dark.

Those lights were not planes. She could see that now. They'd turned violet, and were coalescing below, blending into one long flash.

The plane hummed. Guy hummed too, snoring in his seat.

"Hey," Penny said, "hey," nudging him—her one true love, who only had so much forgiveness left—awake.

"Hey, what is that—" she turned to him, "—out the window?"

Guy would know. He could identify anything. Could name it, define it.

"What is that?" she said.

But when she turned back, the violet light was gone. She could just make out a white blur, trapped in the plastic.

A pale, smudged face. Hair, in a brown-yellow halo. And in the center, a small, white mouth.

It moved.

"What is that?" it asked. "What is that?"